KU-151-798

TARZAN

Introduction

Edgar Rice Burroughs was born in 1875, in Chicago, America. He was the son of a business man. In his early twenties, he worked as a gold miner, a cowboy and a policeman before he became a full-time writer.

He wrote his first adventure stories as serials in weekly magazines.

Burroughs wrote *Tarzan of the Apes* in 1914, when he was thirty nine years old. It tells the story of a baby – orphaned in the African jungle – who was brought up by apes, not knowing that his parents were Lord and Lady Greystoke of England.

Ten years later, Burroughs wrote another famous book: *The Land that Time Forgot*. Although he wrote other science fiction books, he is best known for the Tarzan stories. He wrote twenty-three of them.

Burroughs set up his own company and published all his own books. Tarzan became big business: he appeared in a comic strip, on the radio, in many films – and eventually on television.

Edgar Rice Burroughs even called his ranch in California *Tarzana* – and he died there in 1950, at the age of seventy-five.

CHAPTER ONE

The white ape

One sunny morning in 1888, a young man called John
Clayton – Lord Greystoke – sailed from England to work
in West Africa. When he and his wife Alice reached Africa,
they boarded a boat to take them further along the coast.

They never arrived.

The sailors stole the boat and left the young couple on a
deserted beach close to the jungle. Lord and Lady
Greystoke watched them row away.

'Oh John!' Alice Clayton cried. 'What are we going to
do? What about the child we are expecting?'

'Somebody will come searching for us,' her husband
replied. 'And while we wait, we must be brave, Alice.'

There were trees close to the beach. Clayton tied some
of their branches together to make a platform between
them, with a roof and walls. By dusk, they were safe in
their tree room, watching the darkening shadows of the
jungle. Alice grasped her husband's arm.

'John! Look!' she whispered. 'What is that? Is it a
man?'

Clayton turned to look. He saw a tall figure on a hill,
silhouetted against the moon.

'It is only a shadow,' he replied.

Clayton kept watch all night, clutching his rifle and
revolvers and listening to the screams of wild animals.

The sailors had left them with all their belongings:
boxes full of clothes and books and tools, as well as biscuits

and a barrel of fresh water. The next day, after breakfast, Clayton started to build a small cabin about a hundred yards from the beach. Soon they were comfortable there and they even slept well at night.

In the following weeks, Clayton and his wife caught sight of tall man-like creatures, like the one they had seen that first night. But they never came close to their cabin.

One afternoon, when Clayton was chopping down a tree, he caught sight of a large shape making its way towards him. It was an ape, growling as it moved.

'Go inside, Alice!' he called.

He started to swing his axe at the beast.

As she entered the cabin, his wife looked back in terror. The ape was now standing between the cabin and Clayton. It was an enormous male with nasty, close set eyes. He bared his great fangs in a horrible snarl.

The ape snatched the axe from Clayton's hands and hurled it away. Alice picked up a revolver and fired. The ape ran roaring towards her. Then it fell to the ground, dead.

That night, a son was born in that tiny cabin. Lady Greystoke never recovered from the shock of the great ape's attack. She never went outside the cabin again.

John Clayton did all he could to make her life comfortable. Animal skins warmed the floors and walls. Clay vases held beautiful flowers. Curtains of bamboo and grass covered the windows. He read to his wife and child from the books they had brought from England. During this time, Clayton wrote a diary in French of their strange life, which he kept in a little metal box.

In the following year, great apes attacked them many times, but Clayton always carried a gun and he always killed them.

***

In the jungle, old Kerchak, the king of the apes was angry. He was the biggest ape of the tribe. And in his tribe, there were eight ape families – about seventy apes in all.

Kerchak was thinking about that animal on the beach with the thunder-stick, the animal that often killed members of his tribe. How he wanted to sink his teeth into its neck!

As he paced up and down, he caught sight of a young ape called Kala. She was returning from a search for food with her baby – her first child. When she saw how angry Kerchak was, she jumped into the next tree. But the leap loosened the baby at her neck and it fell to the ground thirty feet below.

Kerchak ordered the apes to follow him to the beach. Kala carried her dead baby on her breast. At noon, they reached the ridge overlooking the tiny cabin.

That same morning, Lady Alice did not wake up. She had died in her sleep. John Clayton wept for her and wrote in his diary: *"My little son is crying for his milk. O Alice, Alice, what shall I do?"*

As he wept for his wife, the apes crept forward. They opened the door of the cabin and went in. Clayton rose from the table and faced them. But Kerchak squeezed the life out of him. Kala ran to the crying baby and picked it up, dropping the body of her dead baby into the cradle.

Hunger worked its charm. Soon the son of an English lord and an English lady was feeding at the breast of Kala the ape. She named her baby Tarzan, which meant 'white skin.' Kala nursed her little orphan and wondered why he was not as strong as the other baby apes. How stupid he was! He could not even find his own food.

Her husband, Tublat – whom everybody called Broken Nose – hated Tarzan.

'He will never be a great ape,' he grumbled to Kala.

'You will always have to look after him. Leave him to die.'

'No, Broken Nose!' she replied.

By the time Tarzan was ten years old, he was more cunning than his brothers and sisters, although he was smaller and less strong than them. But he could swing from branch to branch like them, and drop twenty feet at a time to the ground. He could plait ropes from the creepers. He was happy because he had known no other life.

But Tarzan was starting to realise that he was different from the other apes. He was ashamed because he was hairless. One day, he went to a little lake to drink with one of his cousins. As he leaned over the water, he noticed his reflection for the first time

He was shocked. 'I knew that my body was hairless!' he thought, 'but look at my teeth! They are *so* small. And my nose is pinched and thin. I wish I had wide nostrils like the others.'

As he stared at himself, he did not hear Sabor, the lioness, creeping towards them – not until she roared. His cousin froze in horror as the lioness pounced on him. Tarzan, because he was a human being, was able to think, 'I would be safer in the water.'

So Tarzan jumped into the lake, although he could not swim! By splashing his arms and legs, he stayed afloat. Then Tarzan raised his voice in the call for help used by the apes. Forty or fifty of them came rushing through the trees to chase Sabor away.

From then on, Tarzan enjoyed swimming every day. Kala watched him in surprise because apes do not like water, except to drink.

And from that day, Tarzan *never* forgot that Sabor was his enemy.

CHAPTER TWO

Reading and writing

Tarzan's tribe of apes roamed twenty-five miles along the coast and about fifty miles inland to find food. They often came close to the silent cabin by the sea. The other apes kept their distance, remembering the thunder-stick. But Tarzan was not afraid.

One day, he went in.

He stared in astonishment. In the middle of the floor lay a skeleton. On the bed was another – and a tiny skeleton lay in the cradle. Tarzan was used to seeing dead animals and he was not upset.

He examined everything: strange tools and weapons, paper, clothing – and in a cupboard, a book with brightly coloured pictures. Under the pictures were black marks that looked like insects: **A is for Archer...B is for Boy....M is for Monkey**. He did not find a picture that looked like Kala or Kerchak. But he found a picture of Sabor under **L is for Lion**.

Tarzan looked at the book until it was almost dark. Then he locked it away again, picked up a knife and left. He had never enjoyed himself so much!

As Tarzan stepped back into the jungle, an enormous shape loomed from the shadows. It was Bolgani, the huge gorilla and gorillas were the great enemy of his tribe.

'There is no time to run,' Tarzan thought. 'Now I shall have to fight for my life.'

Tarzan beat the gorilla's body with his fists, and by

chance, he caught him with the blade of the knife. Bolgani shrieked with pain. Tarzan thrust the knife again and again into its body as they rolled on the ground.

Kala, hearing the sound of battle, came to help. In the moonlight, she found Tarzan's torn little body and beside him, the dead gorilla.

It took Tarzan many days to recover his strength. And as soon as he could, he went back to find the knife. He knew that it was a useful new weapon. Then he decided to go inside the cabin again to look at the picture book.

Tarzan squatted on the table top in his father's cabin, his smooth brown body bent over the book, his long black hair falling over his eyes. In this way, he learned to read.

From the dictionary, he leaned that he was a man. Now he was no longer ashamed of his hairless body and his human face.

***

The other apes knew that Tarzan was different. The older males took no notice of him. Some of them hated him – his father, Tublat, most of all. But one day, when he was about thirteen, Tarzan earned the respect of the tribe.

That day, the apes had gathered in an open space to celebrate the killing of a great enemy ape. Kerchak beat his breast with his hairy paws. His terrible shriek rang out across the land. Then the apes danced around the dead beast before they began to eat it.

Tarzan used his knife to cut off a whole forearm and took it into a tree. Tublat followed Tarzan to steal his meat, but he could not reach him. Tublat went mad with rage and attacked some of the females, including Kala. Tarzan hurried down the tree and threw himself in between them.

With a roar, Tublat leaped upon little Lord Greystoke, but his fangs never tore his flesh. Tarzan plunged the knife into Tublat's hairy throat. Then he placed his foot on the neck of his lifelong enemy, threw back his head and beat his breast.

'I am Tarzan!' he screamed in their language. 'I am Tarzan of the apes!'

***

Nothing changed in Tarzan's wild life for several years. He grew stronger and wiser. He learned from his books about the strange world that lay outside his jungle.

He hunted the animals, and sometimes they hunted him. He made friends with Tantor, the elephant and often rode upon his back. Sometimes, he came across his enemy Sabor and tried to catch her with his rope. But she always escaped.

By the time he was seventeen, Tarzan could read all the books in the cabin. He found pencils, too, and copied the words. By the age of eighteen, he was an English lord who could speak no English, yet he could read and write it. He had never seen another human being because high hills shut off the jungle on three sides, and the ocean on the other.

But one day, Tarzan's safe life disappeared for ever.

CHAPTER THREE

King of the apes

The Mbonga tribe was running away from the white men who had come to Africa to look for rubber and ivory. Now they had built a new village close to Kerchak's tribe.

Kala, hunting for food, came face to face with Kulonga, the chief's son. He fired a poisoned arrow at her and she plunged to the ground with a loud scream.

Tarzan, hearing the noise, knew that something terrible had happened. He found the apes screeching around the body of his dead mother. He roared and beat his chest with his fists and fell across her body. He sobbed. Tarzan felt the same love for her that any boy would feel for his mother.

Then Tarzan sped through the tree-tops, clutching his hunting-knife and rope. His heart beat fast.

'A is for Archer,' he thought. 'The arrow in Kala's body is like the one in my picture book. Am I hunting somebody like me – a man?'

After about a mile, Tarzan came across Kulonga. He was about to shoot his arrow at a wild boar. Tarzan looked at him in amazement – they were so alike, except for the other man's face and colour.

To Tarzan's surprise, the small wooden stick killed the boar. Kulonga cut its flesh with a knife, built a fire and cooked it. Tarzan had never seen fire, except when lightning sometimes destroyed a tree.

'How can this man make red and yellow fangs that turn wood to dust?' he asked himself. 'I must watch and learn.'

Tarzan followed Kulonga all that day. And that night, he crept down from his tree and stole his bow and arrows. Then he tracked Kulonga again. He wanted to find out where he had come from.

Suddenly, they came to a clearing.

In it stood a village of thatched huts, surrounded by fields of plants. Quickly, before Kulonga could leave the jungle, Tarzan threw the rope around his neck. Then he dragged him back into the trees and killed him.

Tarzan's savage life had taught him only one thing: these other people were enemies. To kill was the law of the world in which he had lived.

'Now I have punished my mother's killer,' he thought.

He lowered Kulonga to the ground. Then, curious, he made his way to a part of the jungle that was closer to the thatched huts.

He watched. Naked children played outside. Women were grinding dried grass and other women gathered plants in the fields. They wore grass around their hips, and metal around their arms and necks and in their noses.

A woman worked right under the tree where Tarzan was crouching. She was dipping arrows into a thick, red liquid. Tarzan knew nothing of poison, but he knew that a small arrow could not have killed the wild boar. His intelligence told him that this liquid was to blame.

Suddenly, he heard a loud cry coming from the place where he had killed Kulonga. Everybody left their work and ran to see what had happened.

Tarzan took his chance. He dropped from the tree, picked up a bow and some arrows, and hurried away from the village of Mbonga.

Tarzan practised hard until he leaned how to shoot an arrow straight. But soon his arrows were all used up.

'I shall have to go back to the black man's village,' he thought.

During this time, Tarzan found something else that was important, too. At the back of a cupboard in the cabin, he found a small metal box. Inside was a photograph of a young man, a locket on a gold chain and a small book full of writing he could not read.

He put the locket around his neck, like the men and women in the village did, and put the other things back in the cupboard.

'One day, I shall read those strange words,' he said to himself.

***

It was time for Tarzan to go back to the village for more arrows. He waited all day in the tree above the pot of boiling liquid, but the woman did not leave it. As darkness fell, the workers returned from the fields. Then the warriors returned from the forest, carrying a struggling animal.

When they came closer, Tarzan saw that they were carrying a man. The women and children beat him with sticks and stones and tied him to a wooden post.

Tarzan was sad. 'How cruel my fellow men are!' he thought. 'Even the wild animals kill their victims quickly.'

The people began to dance around the terrified man.

'I hope that they do not eat him alive,' Tarzan thought. 'Apes do not do that!

But the dance gave Tarzan the chance he wanted. He dropped to the ground and gathered up the arrows. But he wanted these people to know that he had been there. He slipped into one of the huts, picked up a skull and climbed into the tree. Then he hurled the skull into the group of people and they ran about, shrieking with terror.

As he made his way back to his tribe, Tarzan came face to face again with his enemy, Sabor. Her great yellow eyes were fixed on him, and she licked her lips with longing.

Tarzan did not try to escape.

'Now I have a better weapon than a rope or a knife,' he thought.

He fired an arrow into Sabor's top leg. With a roar, Sabor charged again. Tarzan fired another arrow and she fell to the ground, dead.

Tarzan placed a foot upon the body of his enemy and roared. The sound echoed through the forest and the other animals crept away. None of them ever looked for trouble with the great white ape.

When Tarzan returned to his tribe, he proudly carried Sabor's skin.

'Look what the mighty Tarzan has done!' he cried from the top of a tree.

Kerchak was full of anger and envy.

'Come down, Tarzan!' he shrieked. 'Come down and feel my fangs! Great killers do not hide in trees!'

Quietly, Tarzan dropped to the ground.

As Kerchak came roaring towards him, Tarzan met the attack with a bloodcurdling roar. He grasped Kerchak's wrist and plunged his knife below his heart. The ape's teeth were only an inch from Tarzan's neck when he suddenly stiffened and fell down dead. Tarzan pulled out his knife, placed his foot on Kerchak's neck and gave his ear-splitting cry of triumph.

And so the young Lord Greystoke became the king of the apes.

CHAPTER FOUR

Tarzan decides

There was one ape who did not accept Tarzan – Terkoz, the son of Tublat and Kala – and Tarzan's ape brother. But he was afraid of Tarzan's knife and deadly arrows.

The tribe was happy because Tarzan was an intelligent hunter. At night, he led them to the villagers' fields and stole their crops, while he stole more arrows.

The villagers were afraid of the enemy they could not see. They moved further into the jungle to build a new village. Now the jungle was filled with men's voices.

The great apes wanted to move away, but Tarzan hated the thought of leaving the little cabin. However, one day the black men built their huts on the banks of the river where the apes drank. Tarzan led his tribe deeper into the jungle – but he still came back to the sea from time to time to steal arrows and read his books.

He had one great fear: that these men would find his cabin.

So Tarzan spent less and less time with his tribe. He was tired of being king. He longed to be alone in the cool house by the sea.

'I have grown apart from my people,' he thought. 'I do not share their interests, and I cannot share all the wonderful things I have discovered in my books.'

But Tarzan was stubborn.

'I shall not leave yet,' he thought, 'because Terkoz is waiting to become king in my place. No, I shall not run away from my enemy.'

One day, the matter was suddenly decided. The tribe was feeding quietly when Terkoz began to beat an old female ape. He knew that her husband was too weak to defend her. Tarzan warned him to stop, but Terkoz carried on. Tarzan threw himself upon his enemy.

Never had he fought such a battle since that day he had fought Bolgani, the great gorilla. Soon they were rolling on the ground, tearing at each other.

Tarzan of the apes – the young Lord Greystoke – would have died except for one thing: he could think about what he would do next. As soon as Terkoz stopped to catch his breath, Tarzan climbed onto his back. There he was safe from those terrible fangs. Then he pulled Terkoz' arms behind his back and pulled him to the ground.

'I could break his neck easily,' Tarzan thought, 'but as long as he is alive, he will be an example to the other apes not to challenge me.'

'*Kagoda*?' Tarzan asked in their language. '*Do you surrender?*'

'*Kagoda!*' his enemy shrieked.

'Next time I shall kill you,' Tarzan said. 'Do you understand?'

'Huh,' Terkoz agreed.

The apes went back to their feeding. But deep inside their minds they knew that their king was a strange creature. He had had the power to kill his enemy – but he had allowed him to live.

At dusk, as the tribe came together to sleep, Tarzan called the males to him.

'You have seen today that Tarzan is great,' he said. 'But Tarzan is not an ape. He is not like his tribe. So he is going back to the house of his own people by the water. You must choose another king, because Tarzan will not return.'

The following morning, Tarzan, limping and sore from his fight, set out for the sea. He reached the cabin the next day. His wounds slowly healed, leaving a terrible scar above his left eye which ran down to his ear.

'I must have clothes,' Tarzan thought. 'That is what will make me a man rather than an ape.'

From that day, Tarzan kept the skins and ornaments from the black warriors he killed. A bow and arrows hung from his shoulder and a leather belt held his knife. The golden chain which held the locket hung around his neck.

Tarzan hated the hair that had begun to grow on his face – like the apes had. He did not want to be like them. And so, with his knife, he learned to shave.

He was a strange sight: strong and straight, a hunter, a warrior, but intelligence shone in his eyes.

In all these ways, the young Lord Greystoke was taking the first steps towards the life that he wanted – to be like the men he had seen in his picture book.

CHAPTER FIVE

His own people

One day, as Tarzan was returning to his cabin, he saw something he had never seen before. A ship called the *Arrow* lay off the coast, and on the beach stood a small boat. White men were walking along the beach. They were like the pictures in his book – and like himself.

Tarzan crept behind the trees to watch.

There were ten men, all talking loudly and shaking their fists. One of them, a small man with a face like a rat, put his hand on the shoulder of the tall man next to him. He pointed inland and the man turned to look. The small man took out his revolver and shot him in the back.

The sound of the shot amazed Tarzan, although he was not afraid. But he did not like the behaviour of the men.

'They are as cruel as the black warriors,' he thought.

Soon afterwards, the men climbed into the boat and rowed back to the ship. Tarzan slipped into his cabin and found that it had been searched. Anger rose in him. He ran to the cupboard, took out the little metal box and breathed a sigh of relief.

The photograph of the smiling young man was safe – and the book with the strange writing.

A loud noise made Tarzan look through the window. People were climbing from the big ship into small boats. Tarzan picked up a pencil and a piece of paper, wrote on it and fixed it to the door of the cabin. Then, picking up his precious box, his arrows and as many spears as he could

carry, he disappeared into the forest.

Five people were brought ashore that day: an elderly man with white hair and spectacles called Professor Porter; his nineteen year old daughter called Jane; her companion and nurse, Esmeralda; a tall young man dressed in white called Cecil Clayton (the son of John Clayton's younger brother) and Professor Porter's assistant, a fussy old man called Mr Philander.

The group walked in silence up to the cabin door and stared at this notice:

THIS IS THE HOUSE OF TARZAN, they read, **THE KILLER OF BEASTS AND BLACK MEN. TARZAN IS WATCHING YOU.**

TARZAN OF THE APES

Tarzan could not understand what the people were saying, but he saw that the rat-faced sailor was quarrelling with the young man. As the two older men walked off into the jungle, the sailor pointed his revolver at him. The young woman screamed a warning.

At the same time, a spear flew from the trees and hit the sailor in the right shoulder. He dropped his revolver and collapsed.

'Who threw that spear?' Jane whispered to Clayton.

'I am sure that Tarzan of the apes is not very far away,' he replied. 'Take Esmeralda and lock yourselves inside the cabin while I find your father.'

When they were safely inside, Esmeralda searched for something to barricade the door. As she looked around the cabin for the first time, a shriek of terror rose to her lips.

On the floor lay the whitened skeleton of a man. Then

they saw the other on the bed, and the tiny one in the cradle.

'What horrible place have we come to?' Jane whispered.

Clayton picked up the spear and plunged into the jungle in search of his friends. The sailors took the boats and went back to the ship where they would be safe from the unseen spears.

'I trust the men who have gone into the jungle,' Tarzan thought, 'but I do not trust the sailors.'

Tarzan's head was in a whirl with all the wonders he had seen that day. But the most wonderful sight had been the face of the beautiful young girl.

CHAPTER SIX

Danger in the jungle

Tarzan wanted to help Clayton. He followed him into the jungle. Suddenly, he caught sight of a yellow glint in the leaves moving towards the young man.

It was Sheeta, the leopard. As she crouched, ready to spring, Tarzan ran forward, giving a warning cry. Sheeta ran away.

Clayton's blood ran cold when he realised what had happened. But he did not know that his own cousin, the real Lord Greystoke, had saved his life that day. Now he thought only of the woman he loved – Jane. He ran back towards the cabin to protect her. He did not realise that he was going the wrong way – towards Mbonga's village.

'No man should go to that village,' Tarzan thought. 'And I can see a lion stalking him.'

Clayton had heard the lion, too. He turned to face the bushes, spear in his hand, trembling in the dusk.

'I shall die here alone, torn apart by a wild beast,' he said to himself.

Then Clayton heard a noise in the tree above him. He dare not look up. As he kept his eyes on the lion, he saw an arrow sink into its body. With a roar of pain, the beast sprang. At the same time, a huge man dropped from the tree onto the lion's back. He pulled the animal's front paws from the ground and stabbed him over and over again with his knife.

The man flung the dead lion down. Then he placed his

foot on its body and gave a loud cry.

'Thank you,' Clayton said to the stranger in English. 'I have never seen anybody so strong.'

Tarzan shrugged his shoulders and bent down to cut flesh from the lion. He began to eat, pointing to Clayton to join him. But he shook his head.

'If this man is Tarzan of the Apes,' Clayton thought,' and if he wrote that note in English, he *must* be able to speak English.'

Clayton spoke again; but Tarzan only grunted in reply.

'It is not him,' Clayton thought, disappointed.

As Tarzan led Clayton back to the cabin, they heard the sound of a revolver shot. Then there was silence. Tarzan pulled Clayton quickly onto his back and climbed into the trees. Clayton's fear turned to amazement as they moved through the darkening shadows, more than a hundred feet above the ground.

'I shall *never* forget this,' he thought.

Soon they came to the cabin. A lion was trying to squeeze itself through the window, although Jane had wounded it with a bullet. Then she had fainted. Esmeralda was cowering in a corner.

Jane opened her eyes in time to see an ape-man pulling the lion by its tail back through the window. Tarzan told Clayton to shoot poisoned arrows into the animal, or take the knife from his belt to stab him; but he did not understand.

Tarzan, remembering his fight with Terkoz, his ape-brother, threw himself onto the lion's back. He pulled its paws up so that it fell over. Then he broke its neck. Tarzan leapt to his feet, giving his roar of victory. Then he disappeared into the jungle before anybody could thank him.

'Who was that?' Jane asked Clayton, trembling. 'A human being cannot have uttered such a shriek!'

'It was the cry of the kill from the man who has saved our lives!' he replied. 'But he cannot be Tarzan because he does not understand my English.'

'He has saved our lives,' Jane said, 'whoever he is.'

***

Several miles south of the cabin, on a sandy beach, Professor Porter was arguing with Mr Philander. They were lost. All around them, animals roared and growled. A lion came close.

'Tut, tut!' the Professor grumbled. 'I have never seen one of these animals allowed to roam outside its cage. I shall report it to the zoo keeper.'

Mr Philander led him away, but the lion followed them.

The two men started to run. From the trees, Tarzan watched, grinning. He knew that the lion would not attack them because it had just eaten. But if one of them tripped over, it might kill for fun.

Tarzan swung onto a lower branch, and pulled up the men by their coat collars as they hurried past.

'Thank you, Mr Philander,' the Professor said. 'You saved my life.'

'No, thank *you*,' Mr Philander replied. '*You* saved mine.'

They looked at each other in silence.

'There must be somebody up here with us,' Mr Philander whispered.

Tarzan, hidden in the tree, let out his terrible roar to frighten the lion away. The two men swayed with fright and fell to the ground. As they got up, they saw Tarzan watching them.

'Good evening, sir,' the professor said, lifting his hat.

Tarzan beckoned them to follow him; but the men started to argue again. Tarzan placed his rope around their necks and led them through the jungle until they reached the cabin. The he slipped away.

'Most remarkable,' the Professor muttered.

Together again at last, the small group told each other of their adventures.

'That wild man must be our guardian angel,' Esmeralda said.

'There was nothing angelic about his voice,' said Jane.

'I do not think an angel would drag two famous scientists through the jungle on a rope,' Professor Porter said.

And they laughed for the first time that day.

CHAPTER SEVEN

Buried treasure

The next morning, the men prepared to bury the skeletons they had found in the cabin. As they wrapped the man in a cloth, Clayton noticed a ring on his finger.

'This is my family crest!' he shouted in surprise. 'This man must be my uncle John, Lord Greystoke. Everybody thought he had drowned at sea.'

'And this must be Lady Greystoke,' Jane said sadly.

The bodies were buried beside the cabin, and between them they placed the little body of their child. As Mr Philander was wrapping the tiny skeleton, he looked at its skull in surprise, but he did not say anything.

From the trees, Tarzan watched the burial – but most of all he watched the sweet face of Jane Porter. He wanted to protect her.

In the distance, the *Arrow* was sailing out to sea. Esmeralda shook her fist.

'They're deserting us!' she cried.

'And they have taken our treasure with them,' Professor Porter said. 'I shall be a ruined man now.'

Tarzan saw the look of worry on their faces.

'I shall go to the north end of the harbour,' he thought. 'Then I can see where that strange floating house is going.'

He swung quickly through the trees until he could see the ship. To his surprise, it was turning back towards the land. Men lowered a large trunk into a rowing boat and they brought it to the beach below Tarzan's tree. There the sailors buried it in the sand and left again.

'Why did they bury the box?' Tarzan thought. 'Why did they not throw it into the sea if they did not want it? Ah, I understand! They *do* want it.'

Tarzan dug up the chest. It had taken four men to carry it to the beach, but he carried it alone to the clearing where the apes met for their celebrations. Here he buried it again.

Tarzan knew that the box must contain something important. Both men and apes are curious and he would have opened it – but even *he* could not break the metal ropes that fastened it.

It was dark by the time Tarzan reached the cabin again. Inside, an oil lamp was burning and Jane was writing at

Tarzan's table by the window. How he wanted to speak to her! When she had put out the lamp and gone to bed, Tarzan reached through the window and took the piece of paper.

Then he disappeared into the jungle as softly as a shadow.

As soon as it was light, Tarzan unrolled the paper. The little black marks, which he knew well from his books, leaned over. Slowly, he was able to read it.

West Coast of Africa
February, 1909

Dear Hazel

You may never read this letter, but I must tell you all the horrible things that have happened since we left England. Papa said we were coming on a scientific expedition – but really he was looking for buried Spanish treasure. He borrowed the money from his friend, Robert Canler.

We found the island – and the treasure!

But it brought terror to us all. The sailors murdered the captain and his officers and they have left us miles from anywhere. And they have stolen our treasure.

Wild animals have attacked us many times, but we have been saved by a strange man who vanishes into the jungle.

Your friend, Jane Porter

Tarzan thought for a long time before he wrote at the

end of the letter:

I am Tarzan of the Apes

Then he put it back exactly where he had found it.

***

A few days later, a woman's scream rang through the jungle. The men found Esmeralda fainting on the ground.

'Where is Miss Porter?' Clayton shouted.

'It took her away!' she sobbed.

'What took her away?' Professor Porter asked.

'A great big giant all covered with hair,' she replied.

'Was it an ape, Esmeralda?' Mr Philander asked.

She nodded.

The men searched the jungle all day long, but they were forced to give up as darkness fell.

Jane had disappeared.

CHAPTER EIGHT

Tarzan and Jane

There had been trouble in the ape tribe ever since Tarzan had left – ever since Terkoz had become king. At last, some of the males fought him and expelled him from their group. Now he wandered in the jungle, full of hatred, until he came upon two women gathering berries. He swung from the tree and snatched Jane. As his fangs closed around her throat, she gave a piercing scream.

Suddenly, Terkoz stopped. 'The tribe has kept my women. I must find others,' he thought. 'This hairless white ape shall be my first.'

He threw Jane across his shoulder and leaped into the trees.

That scream brought Tarzan to where Esmeralda lay. He sped after Terkoz and slowly overtook him. Terkoz dropped to the ground and turned to attack. Then he saw that it was Tarzan who had been following him.

'So I have Tarzan's woman!' he thought. 'Now I can take revenge on my old enemy!'

'Here is my guardian angel once more!' Jane said to herself.

But she was sick with fear when she saw the great muscles and fangs of the ape. Terkoz pushed her aside as he and Tarzan charged each other, trying to reach each other's throats. Tarzan flashed his knife and plunged it straight into Terkoz' heart.

Tarzan looked at Jane. 'I have won her in a fair fight,' he

thought, 'and now she is mine.'

He picked her up and carried her into the jungle. Jane looked up at Tarzan's face. There was no hatred there. He smiled at her, and she felt safe with him.

Tarzan was puzzled. 'It is the law of the jungle for a male to take the female he has saved,' he thought. 'But I am a man! What do men do?'

High in the trees, Tarzan brought Jane fruit, and soft grasses and ferns to lie on. Jane pointed to his locket and he took it off. She opened it and gazed at the two paintings inside: a beautiful woman and a man who looked just like the man beside her. Tarzan looked at them in astonishment. He had not realised that the locket opened.

'Who are they?' his eyes seemed to ask.

'The locket belongs to Lord and Lady Greystoke,' Jane thought. 'This wild creature must have found it on the beach. But why do they look so much alike?'

Tarzan fastened the locket around Jane's neck. Then, as the sun set, he let her sleep, guarding her all night long.

The next morning, Jane's heart beat faster when she saw Tarzan.

'I am so happy that I want to stay here,' she thought.

But Tarzan swept Jane into his arms and swung through the trees. He was taking her back to her own people.

***

That same morning, the booming of a cannon gun woke up the four people in the cabin. Clayton rushed outside and saw a French ship just off the coast. He lit a small fire and the ship turned round. A boat brought men to the beach, led by a young French officer called D'Arnot.

When they heard what had happened to Jane, D'Arnot insisted on forming a search party. Within a few minutes, they were entering the jungle with Professor Porter and Cecil Clayton.

Not far from Mbonga's village, the warriors ambushed them. Many men were killed in the fight that followed, and they took D'Arnot prisoner. The others decided to return to the beach for help.

As Tarzan and Jane arrived at the cabin, they heard the shots of the fight far off in the jungle. Leaving Jane with Mr Philander and Esmeralda, Tarzan swung through the trees straight towards the village of Mbonga.

'If men have survived, they will be tied to that stake,' he told himself. 'But will I be too late?'

Night had now fallen and the moon lit up his path through the tree tops.

Tarzan was right. From a tree, he watched the Mbonga warriors dancing in the firelight around a man tied to a stake. One of them, holding a spear, leapt in front of the terrified man.

Tarzan threw his noose, caught the warrior around his neck and pulled him into the air. Then he dropped from a tree and, without a word, he cut the man's ropes and lifted him into the trees.

CHAPTER NINE

Learning to speak

When the rest of the search party reached the cabin again, they were relieved to see Jane. Clayton was happy. The woman he loved was safe.

'Where is man who saved me?' Jane asked.

'Who do you mean?' Clayton said.

'The jungle man who saved me,' Jane replied. 'Then he came to help you all.'

'We did not see him,' Clayton said. 'Perhaps he has gone back to his own tribe – the men who attacked us. They have killed many Frenchmen and captured their officer.'

'No, he could not be one of them,' Jane said. 'He is too kind.'

'He is a creature of the jungle, Miss Porter,' Clayton replied. 'He *must* belong to one of the tribes.'

Jane turned pale. 'No,' she whispered. 'That is not true.'

The next morning, Clayton and two hundred men from the French ship set off to search for D'Arnot. They went straight to the village, but they found no trace of him, only scraps of his uniform.

They came back without him.

'We were too late,' Clayton told Jane. 'And it is clear that the Mbonga have eaten him. When your jungle man left you, I expect he was hurrying to the feast.'

Jane held her head high. 'No, Mr Clayton,' she said coldly. '*I* know that he is a gentleman.'

***

D'Arnot had fallen into a deep sleep on a grass bed in the treetops. When he woke up, Tarzan brought him water and fruit, but he did not reply when D'Arnot spoke to him.

I am Tarzan of the Apes, he wrote. **Who are you? Can you read this language?**

'He is an Englishman!' D'Arnot thought.

Why can't you speak English if you can write it? he wrote.

Tarzan's reply amazed D'Arnot: **I speak only the language of my tribe – the great apes. I have never spoken to a human being, except to Jane Porter.**

She is alive! D'Arnot wrote. **Where is she?**

I have taken her back to her people, Tarzan wrote. **When you are well, I shall take you back to your people.**

A few days later, they returned to the cabin.

But there was no ship waiting out at sea. And the cabin was empty, except for a letter for Tarzan.

To Tarzan of the Apes

Thank you for the use of your cabin. There is another man I want to thank, but he did not come back. I do not know his name. He is a white giant who wore a locket around his neck. If you know him, tell him that I live in America, in the city of Baltimore.

Jane Porter.

42

Tarzan stared at Jane's letter for a long time.

'Jane does not know that I am Tarzan of the Apes,' he thought sadly. 'I shall never see her again.'

As they were thinking about what to do next, D'Arnot decided to teach Tarzan some words of English and French.

'Have you *any* idea who you are?' D'Arnot asked.

'My mother was an ape,' Tarzan replied.

'That is not possible,' D'Arnot said.

Tarzan brought out the diary with the strange writing and showed it to D'Arnot. When he had finished reading it, he looked at Tarzan.

'*You* were that baby, Tarzan,' he said. 'You are Lord Greystoke.'

Tarzan shook his head. 'No, that child is buried with its parents,' he replied.

'His fingerprints would prove it,' D'Arnot thought.

Aloud, he asked, 'What are you going to do?'

'Where is America?' Tarzan replied.

'Many thousands of miles across the ocean,' D'Arnot replied. 'Why?'

'I am going there,' Tarzan said.

CHAPTER TEN

To America

In America, Jane had gone to spend some time on her family farm. Clayton was there, too, and he asked Jane to marry him.

'I do not love you enough,' she told him.

'Are you going to marry Robert Canler?' he asked.

Jane shivered. He was the man who had lent her father money for the expedition to Africa – and now he wanted Jane to marry him because her father could not pay him back.

'No!' she replied.

One week later, Robert Canler drove up to the farmhouse. He asked Jane again to marry him at once. At last, to help her father, she agreed and he drove off to fetch a preacher and a wedding license.

Jane decided to go for a last walk in the forest around the farm. She did not see the black smoke rising from a small fire to the east. Suddenly, the wind changed direction and blew the flames towards her.

At the same time, a stranger was driving up to the farmhouse looking for Jane.

'Where is Miss Porter?' this man asked Clayton. He spoke with a French accent. 'Don't you realise you are surrounded by a forest fire?'

Esmeralda pointed to the forest, sobbing.

'Leave now, by the north road,' the man said. 'I shall go and find Jane.'

Although they did not know the stranger, each one of them felt they could trust him.

'Most remarkable!' Professor Porter said.

As Jane tried to reach home, the fire was blocking every path. She was trapped! At last, she stopped running and knelt down to pray. Suddenly, somebody called her name.

'Here! Here!' Jane shouted back.

Through the branches of a tree, she saw a man swinging towards her through the smoke. Then a strong arm lifted her up. Jane glimpsed the ground far below as the man carried her through the trees.

'I must be dreaming about Africa,' she thought.

She glanced up at the man's face. 'My jungle man!' she exclaimed. 'I am *not* dreaming!'

'Yes, I am that man,' Tarzan replied. 'I am the wild man who has come from the jungle to find you!'

'What is your name?' Jane asked.

'I am Tarzan of the Apes,' he replied. 'And I have searched everywhere for you. They told me in Baltimore that a man called Canler has come here to marry you. Is it true?'

She nodded.

'But if your father found the treasure, you would not have to marry him, would you?' Tarzan asked.

'No,' Jane said.

'If you were free, would you marry *me*, Jane?'

'I do not know,' she replied sadly.

'Do you love me?' Tarzan asked.

'Yes, but you would be happier without me, Tarzan,' Jane said. 'You would soon long for the freedom of your old life.'

They met up with the others at a small hotel on the road. Here Robert Canler found them – and with him was a

preacher. Jane begged for more time to think, but he took her by the arm.

Suddenly, a strong arm gripped Canler's arm – and another hand closed around his throat. Jane glanced at Tarzan, horrified, and remembered the day Tarzan had killed the ape that had captured her.

'No, Tarzan,' she said, 'for my sake.'

'Do you promise not to marry Jane?' Tarzan asked Canler.

Canler, gasping for breath, nodded. Professor Porter was angry.

'Why did you interfere?' he asked Tarzan.

'Jane does not love him, sir,' he replied. 'I have found your treasure and brought it here. She does not need to marry him now.'

'Who would have thought it possible?' Mr Philander said. 'The last time I saw you, you were a wild man swinging through the branches of the jungle. Now look at you!'

Tarzan smiled. 'Mr Philander, do you remember anything strange about those skeletons in my cabin?'

'Why do you ask?' Philander said.

'It means a great deal to me and will clear up a mystery,' Tarzan replied. 'Were they all human skeletons?'

'No,' Mr Philander replied. 'The small one was an ape.'

'Thank you,' Tarzan said. 'Now I understand.'

'And soon D'Arnot will send the results of my fingerprint test,' he thought. 'Then I can tell everybody who I am.'

Jane shivered.

'What do I know about this strange creature?' she asked herself. 'Could I marry a man who has lived in the treetops, a man who has killed men? No!' she decided. 'I shall marry

Clayton after all. That will be the sensible thing to do.'

Later that evening, Tarzan came to speak to Jane alone.

'You are free now, Jane,' he said. 'I have become a civilised man for your sake. I can make you happy. Will you marry me, Jane?'

Jane wept. 'I love you!' she said, 'but it is better that I marry Clayton.'

As the others came into the room, Tarzan gazed through the window. In his mind he saw the waving leaves of a giant tree. And at the top, on a grass mat surrounded by fruit and flowers, sat Jane. They were smiling at each other.

Professor Porter handed a telegram to Tarzan. It had come from France and it read: *Fingerprints prove you are Greystoke ... D'Arnot.*

'I cannot thank you enough, sir,' Clayton was saying. 'You are always saving our lives! Can I ask you one question?' Tarzan nodded. 'How did you come to be living in the jungle?'

Tarzan thought hard before he replied. Clayton, his cousin, was the man who would be Lord Greystoke in his place. He had Tarzan's title, Tarzan's land and the woman he loved. But he would not tell him – for love of Jane.

'I was born there,' he replied. 'And I never knew who my father was.'